# Big Book of
# ELMO
## A Treasury of Stories

RP|KIDS
PHILADELPHIA

Running Press Kids
Hachette Book Group
1290 Avenue of the Americas, New York, NY 10104
www.runningpress.com/rpkids
@RP_Kids

www.sesamestreet.org

Printed in China

First Edition: July 2019

Published by Running Press Kids, an imprint of Perseus Books, LLC, a subsidiary of Hachette Book Group, Inc. The Running Press Kids name and logo is a trademark of the Hachette Book Group.

The Hachette Speakers Bureau provides a wide range of authors for speaking events. To find out more, go to www.hachettespeakersbureau.com or call (866) 376-6591.

The publisher is not responsible for websites (or their content) that are not owned by the publisher.

Print book cover and interior design by Christopher M. Eads.

Library of Congress Control Number: 2018947179

ISBN: 978-0-7624-9447-7 (hardcover)

1010

10 9 8 7 6 5 4 3 2 1

# Table of Contents

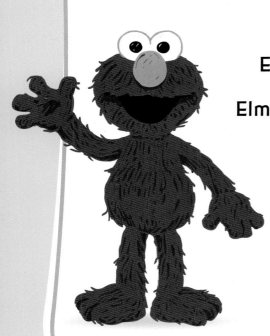

# ELMO'S ABCS

Hello! Elmo is trying to decide
what Elmo's favorite letter is.
Will you help Elmo?

Oh, thank you!

Elmo loves apples
because they are delicious
and crunchy.
And apples start with the letter **A**.
So **A** must be Elmo's favorite letter.

But wait! Baby starts with the letter **B**.
And Elmo loves babies, too. So **B** must
be Elmo's favorite letter. Right, baby?

Crayon and cat begin with the letter **C**.
So Elmo thinks that maybe **C** is Elmo's favorite letter.

Oh, but Elmo LOVES dogs! Hello, doggies! And doggie starts with the letter **D**.

Uh, oh! Elmo just remembered that
Elmo's name begins with the letter **E**.

But Elmo's fur is very fuzzy and fluffy.
So **F** must be Elmo's favorite letter!

But green grapes make a great snack. And grapes begin with the letter **G**!

Coming home for a hug is one
of Elmo's favorite things.

So **H** must be the one.
Ha ha ha! Tee hee hee!

Oh, but Elmo loves to use Elmo's imagination!

And I is the first letter in imagination!

Could it be **J**? Elmo is a very good joke teller.
Would you like to hear Elmo's joke?

**Knock knock.**
Who's there?
**Boo.**
Boo who?
**Please don't cry.**

Elmo just realized
that kangaroo starts
with the letter **K**.

How do you do,
little kangaroo?

Oh, but **L** is the first letter in the
word love. Elmo just loves love!

Monster starts with **M**.
Elmo is a little monster and so are
Elmo's friends.
So **M** must be Elmo's favorite letter.

Elmo can make a lot of noisy noise! Wheeee!!!
And so can an octopus.
Do you think **N** or **O** could be Elmo's favorite letter?

**P** is the first letter in the word poem.
And Elmo just wrote this poem called
"Q is for Quilt."
Is **Q** Elmo's favorite letter?

Q is for quilt.
It's cozy on my bed.
It keeps me
warm and snuggly
From my nose
up to my head.

by
Elmo

Elmo also loves riddles:

What did the sea say to the sand?
Nothing. It just waved.

R must be Elmo's favorite letter!

Can Elmo tell you a secret?
Elmo thinks that you have a very nice smile.
So maybe **S** is Elmo's favorite letter.

Turtles are terrific!
And guess what?
    Turtle begins with a T.

Ha ha ha! Hee hee hee!
Elmo is upside-down.

And Elmo likes to listen
to the violin!

So is Elmo's favorite letter **U**?
Or is it **V**?

Elmo wishes he could decide which is his favorite letter. What about **W**? Or **X**? Could it be **Y**? Why, oh why, can't Elmo decide!

# ELMO'S BIRTHDAY

"Happy birthday, my little monster," said Elmo's mommy as Elmo burst in the door. "Are you all ready for your party?"

"Oh, yes!" said Elmo. "Elmo knows just what Elmo wants! It's cute and black and furry, and it's going to sleep on Elmo's bed every night! This is going to be the best birthday ever!"

Elmo's mommy looked worried as she helped hang the balloons and streamers.

"What's wrong, dear?" asked Elmo's daddy.

"Elmo thinks he is going to get the little black puppy for his birthday," said Elmo's mommy. "You know, the one he has seen all around the neighborhood. But how will we find him? I'd hate to disappoint Elmo."

"A pet would be a nice addition to the family," said Elmo's daddy. "And I think Elmo is ready for the responsibility. Let's see if we can find the little black puppy."

Elmo's parents went downtown to the Sesame Street Pet Shop. Inside, there were turtles and lizards and goldfish and hamsters and mice, but no puppies. Elmo's daddy sighed.

"Now what will we do?" he asked.

"Let's stop at the toy store on the way home," said Elmo's mommy. "There must be something else Elmo would like."

Elmo's mommy and daddy looked at blocks and bikes and basketballs.

"Here's something!" said Elmo's daddy. "It's cute and black and furry and it can sleep on Elmo's bed every night!" Elmo's mommy looked unsure, but she didn't have much choice. The party was about to begin!

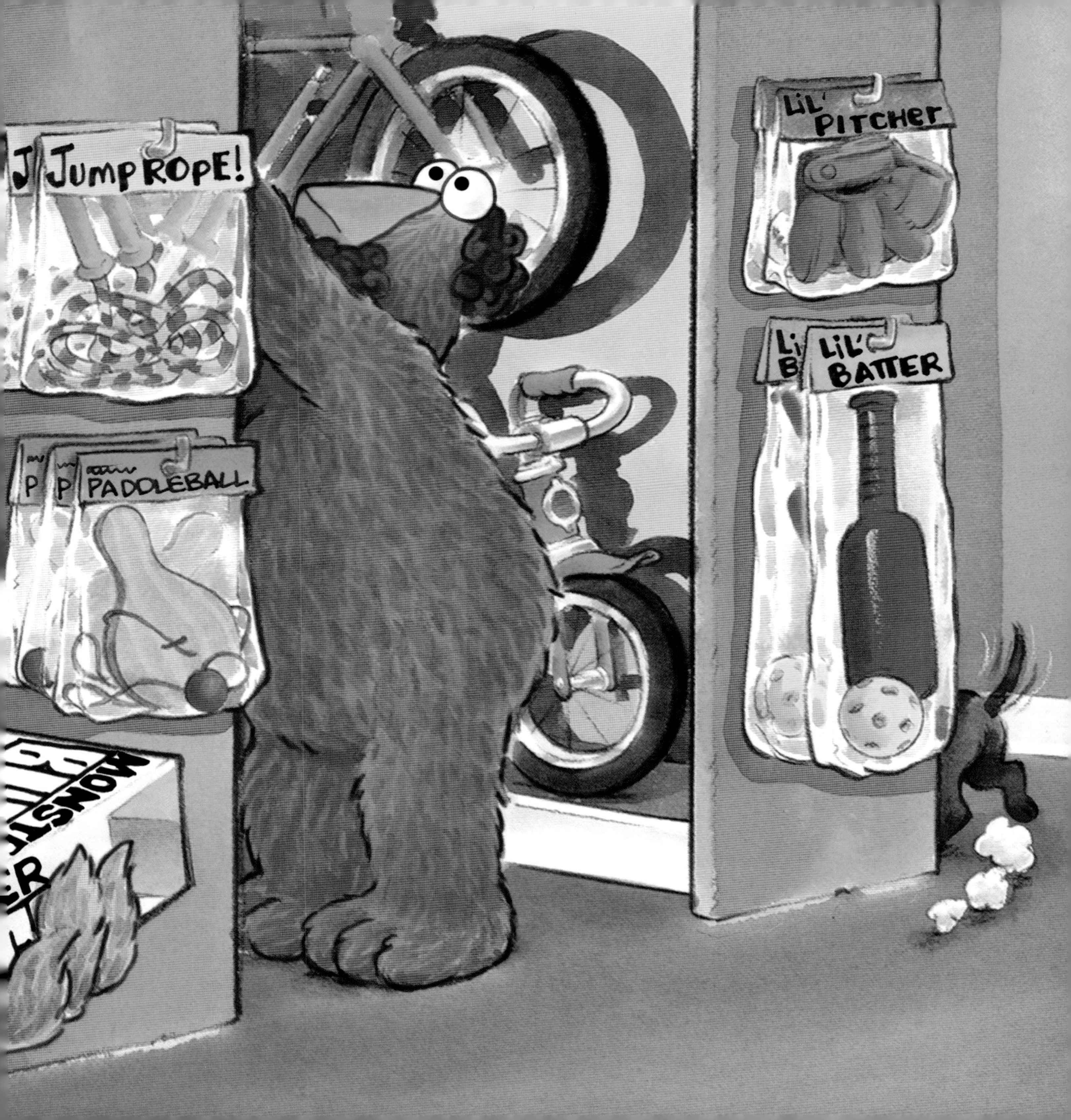
JUMPROPE!
PADDLEBALL
LiL' PITCHER
LiL' BATTER
MONSTER

A little later, Elmo's party guests arrived.
"Hi, Elmo," said Ernie.
"Happy birthday!" said Big Bird.
"Greetings, birthday boy!" said the Count.

Elmo and his friends played Pin the Nose on the
Honker, Monster Freeze Tag, and Blind Monster's Bluff.
Then it was time for ice cream and cake.

"Happy birthday to you!" sang Elmo's friends.
"Make a wish and blow out the candles," said Bert.
"Elmo knows just what to wish for," said Elmo
as he took a deep breath and blew all the candles out.
"Hurray," shouted his friends.
"Now your wish will come true!"
"Time to open your presents!" said Big Bird.

Elmo got a puzzle from Bert, a tie from Big Bird, a toy truck from Zoe, a firefighter's hat from Ernie, a paint set from the Count, and a teddy monster from Herry. Elmo loved his presents, but when was his wish going to come true?

"Happy birthday, Elmo!" said Elmo's parents as they handed him the last present.

123
PAINT WITH ME!
T BY NUMBERS
PAINT BY
MBER
TRAY PUZZLE

Elmo eagerly tore off the wrapping paper.
Inside was a cute, furry, black . . . toy puppy.
"Oh," said Elmo.

Just then, something hopped into Elmo's lap.
"It's Elmo's PUPPY," cried Elmo. "Mommy and Daddy found him!"
"No," laughed his parents. "We think he found you! Happy birthday, little Elmo!"

That night, and every night after that,
the little black puppy slept safe and sound on Elmo's bed.
It was the best birthday ever!

# ELMO GOES TO THE DOCTOR

"Why is Elmo going to visit the doctor today?" Elmo asked one morning, as his mommy buckled the little monster into his car seat. "Elmo doesn't feel sick!"

"It's check-up time," Elmo's mommy reminded him. "You need a check-up even when you feel well. The doctor makes sure you're growing and staying healthy. She'll check your ears and eyes, and listen to your heart, too."

Elmo touched the fuzzy red fur over his heart. "Oooh! Elmo wonders what that sounds like."

"Today you'll find out," Mommy promised.

In the waiting room, Elmo saw a little green monster he knew.
"Lily! Are you here for a check-up, too?"
"No, I have a tummy ache," she said in a small voice,
watching him play with some paper and crayons.
Elmo drew Lily a silly picture to make her smile.
"Will the doctor help Lily feel better?" Elmo asked his mommy.
"I'm sure she will," Mommy answered.

Just then, nurse Rhonda came in. Elmo liked her braided hair. Rhonda smiled a great big smile when she saw Elmo.

"Your turn next, Elmo!" she said.

Later, Elmo followed Rhonda into the examining room.

Rhonda smiled. "Hop up onto the scale, Elmo," she told him. "Let's see how much you've grown."

Rhonda was surprised at how much taller Elmo was since last time. "Elmo is a big monster now," he said happily.

Rhonda checked Elmo's eyes next.

Then she wrapped a cushion around Elmo's arm to test his blood pressure. He watched it puff up and down.

"Just like a balloon!" Elmo giggled.

After that, Dr. Diane came in. She asked Elmo about his pet fish, Dorothy, while she washed her hands.

"Maybe Dorothy needs a check-up, too," Elmo said. "Is there a doctor for fish?"

"Animal doctors are called veterinarians," said Dr. Diane. "But fish don't need check-ups like we do."

Elmo thought about that. "It would be hard to test Dorothy's ears and eyes. They're so tiny!"

"And I would need a scuba suit to give her a check-up," Dr. Diane said with a grin.

That made Elmo laugh!

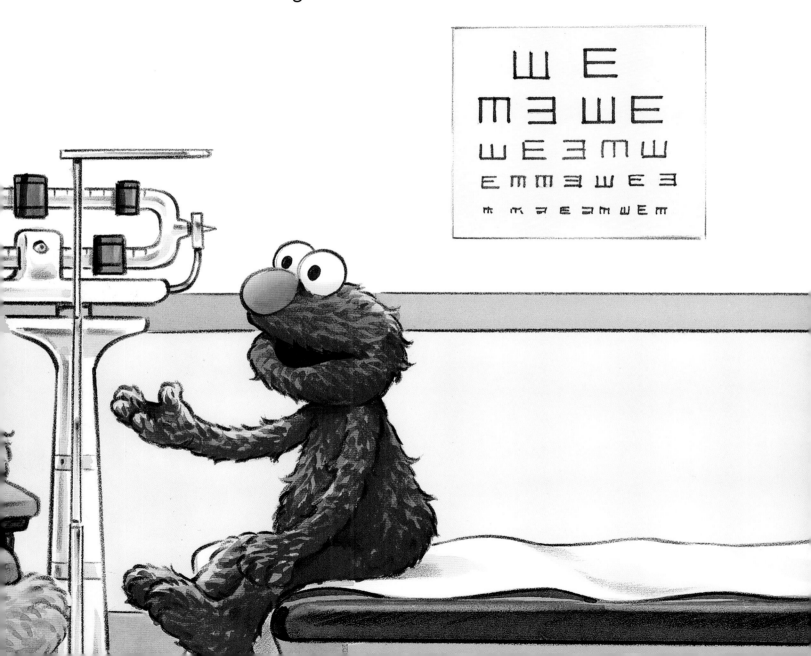

Dr. Diane had a few more tests to give Elmo. She checked his reflexes first. The doctor tap-tap-tapped softly under Elmo's knee until his furry red leg suddenly jumped!

"Ha-ha! That feels so funny," Elmo giggled.

Then she took his temperature with a thermometer.

"Not too hot and not too cold," the doctor said with a smile. "Elmo is just right!"

The doctor checked Elmo's ears with a little light, then his throat. "Open wide, Elmo," she said. Elmo went "aaah."

Next, Dr. Diane asked him to lie down so she could feel his tummy for any aches.

It tickled a little! Elmo tried hard not to giggle until Dr. Diane was through.

Dr. Diane checked Elmo's back, and then said,
"Time to listen to your breathing and your heart, Elmo."

"Yay! Elmo was wondering what a heart sounds like," Elmo exclaimed.

Dr. Diane listened with her stethoscope as Elmo took deep breaths. Then she moved it around to hear Elmo's heart. "This is what I hear," she said.

"Thump-thump. Thump-thump. Thump-thump."

"Elmo's heart sounds like a drum!" said Elmo.

"That's right. Your heart sounds very strong," said Dr. Diane. "Run and play every day and it will get even stronger."

Elmo nodded happily. He could do that!

Finally, Dr. Diane asked Elmo some questions:
"Do you wear a bike helmet to stay healthy and safe? Do you ride in a car seat? Do you make sure a grown-up is watching when you go swimming or cross the street?"
Elmo answered yes to every one.

"And do you get plenty of rest?" the doctor asked Elmo.
He nodded. "Elmo does! And Elmo will make sure
Mommy does, too."
Elmo's mommy laughed at that. "Thank you, Elmo," she said.

"Sometimes we need a shot during a check-up. The medicine keeps us safe from things that make us sick," Dr. Diane said. She looked into a folder with Elmo's name on it. "I see that you need one of those today, Elmo."

Elmo remembered getting a shot one time. He pointed to his arm. "It went right here," Elmo told nurse Rhonda. "It felt like a little pinch, that's all."

Elmo's mommy smiled proudly at Elmo while he got his shot.

"Dr. Diane is good at giving shots," she said, "but you were a very brave monster anyway, Elmo."

That made Elmo feel good. Then Elmo remembered something else.

"Hey, Elmo got a sticker last time!"

Dr. Diane laughed. "You may have a special one today, too."

"Well, Elmo, that's it," said Dr. Diane. "We're done with your check-up."

Elmo waved good-bye happily. He liked knowing he was strong and healthy.

"Thanks, Dr. Diane," he said. "Elmo was feeling okay before his check-up, but now Elmo feels even better!"

**The End**

# ELMO'S COLORFUL ADVENTURE

Hi! Welcome to Elmo's World! Elmo's so happy to see you. Oh, and so is Dorothy. Say hello, Dorothy!

Elmo LOVES to draw pictures. He just drew this picture of Baby David. He's Elmo's very favorite doll. Do you have a favorite toy?

Do you want Elmo to tell you more about Baby David? Great! Elmo will go get him.

Hmm. Elmo's sure Baby David was right here on the table. Baby David?!? Where are you?

Elmo doesn't see Baby David on the table or in the closet or on the floor. Where can he be? Elmo knows! Baby David loves to play games. He must be playing hide-and-seek!

Hmm. Maybe Baby David decided not to hide in Elmo's playroom. Maybe he's somewhere else—like deep inside Dorothy's fishbowl! Do you want to pretend with Elmo and go exploring in Dorothy's fishbowl?

Come on, dive in. The water's fine!

Wow, it's really wet in here! Ooh, and look at all these fish. Dorothy, Elmo had no idea you were so popular!

Elmo sees rocks and coral and plants and an orange drum, but no Baby David. Wait, did Elmo say a DRUM? This looks like the toy drum that Elmo lost last week.

This IS the drum!

So Elmo found something fun, but it isn't Baby David. Elmo doesn't see him anywhere under the water. Elmo wonders—is Baby David ON the water?

Everywhere Elmo looks, he sees blue, like the bright blue sky and the deep blue water. The sky and the water remind Elmo of his favorite crayon. It's called Cookie Monster Blue. Elmo lost it in his backpack. Wait a minute—isn't that Elmo's blue crayon floating by?

Boy, Elmo thought he would never find his blue crayon! But he still wants to find Baby David.

Elmo has an idea. Maybe Baby David's on a lily pad, just like that little frog. Elmo will hop from lily pad to lily pad to look. *Ribbit ribbit. Ribbit ribbit.* No Baby David here, or here, or here. Or anywhere! But there IS something over there. *Ribbit ribbit.*

Hey! It's Elmo's favorite green froggy sunglasses! Elmo thought he lost them!

Elmo found his drum, crayon, and sunglasses in the water. Maybe Elmo will have better luck finding Baby David on land, like here in the place Elmo's imagining now.

Hey, did you know kangaroos hop, just like frogs? Elmo will hippity-hop, too, and look for Baby David.

*Hippity-hop! Hippity-hop! Hippity-hop!*

Elmo sees hills and kangaroos and brown boots, but no Baby David. Hey, wait a minute—what are Elmo's favorite brown boots doing here? He thought he lost them!

*Hippity-hop. Hippity-hop.* Oh, Elmo's feet are tired from all that hippity-hopping. These boots are really made for flying. Elmo can't find Baby David in the water or on the land, so maybe that means he's up in the sky. Up, up, and away!

Elmo doesn't see Baby David up here, but look at all the pretty birds. *Tweet tweet! Tweet tweet!* Elmo sees five birds and one kite. That's the same red kite Elmo lost the other day when he let go of the string!

*Hippity-hop. Hippity-hop.* Oh, Elmo's feet are tired from all that hippity-hopping. These boots are really made for flying. Elmo can't find Baby David in the water or on the land, so maybe that means he's up in the sky. Up, up, and away!

Elmo doesn't see Baby David up here, but look at all the pretty birds. *Tweet tweet! Tweet tweet!* Elmo sees five birds and one kite. That's the same red kite Elmo lost the other day when he let go of the string!

Birds, a kite—Elmo imagines lots of things flying
in the sky! What do YOU see? Do you see Baby David?

No? Then Elmo will keep looking higher up. He can see lots of things
from way up here, like a black hat in that tree.

Hey, that's Elmo's favorite cowboy hat! He almost didn't see it,
covered with all those butterflies. Elmo's not even going to think about
how it got up HERE!

Hi, butterflies! May Elmo have his hat back, please?

Elmo's flown so high that he's floating! Can you guess where Elmo is now? That's right, he's in space!

Elmo's looking behind each and every star up here, and he still can't find Baby David. But Elmo's found something else—a banana! It's just like the one he left behind in his backpack.

Elmo really wants to find Baby David, but Elmo's happy to find his yummy yellow banana. All this swimming, hopping, flying, and floating has made Elmo hungry.

NOW where is Elmo in space? There are a lot of craters on the ground. Ooh, Elmo knows! He's on the moon! Wow, Elmo can see for miles and miles.

Elmo's pretty sure that Baby David's not up here. Nothing unusual on the moon—except for that white spot over there. It's a baseball! Hey, that's the one Elmo hit out of the ballpark the other day! Zoe said it flew so high it must have landed on the moon. It looks like she was right!

Elmo's back in Elmo's World now. What an adventure! Elmo's been swimming in the water, hopping on the land, flying in the sky, and floating in space. Elmo even walked on the moon! And still Elmo has not found Baby David.

Wait—do you think Elmo should look for Baby David in the TOY BOX?

BABY DAVID! Elmo's so happy he found you! Boy, you
missed a really exciting trip in Elmo's imagination. He can't wait to tell
you all about it!

Now it's Elmo's turn to hide. This time, Elmo will hide
with Baby David, and you—you can find us! Close your
eyes and count to ten.

One . . . two . . .
three . . . four . . .
five . . . six . . .
seven . . .
eight . . .
nine . . . ten.
Pretend!

# ELMO'S FURRY FRIEND

At home, Elmo and his parents make his new puppy
feel comfortable and happy.

Elmo learns to take good care of his new pet.

Exercise is important for monster friends and puppy friends!

Elmo and Pal do lots of things together.

Elmo and Pal are the best of friends!

# ELMO VISITS THE DENTIST

"Ow-ow-owooooo!" howled the Big Bad Wolf one day.
"I just want to huff and puff and—and—blow something in!" He plopped
down on a bench, rubbing his chinny-chin-chin.
    "What's wrong, Big Bad?" asked one of the three little pigs.
    "I have a toooooothache!" the wolf complained.

"The dentist helps to take care of Elmo's teeth," said Elmo. "Elmo is pretty sure the dentist can help wolf teeth, too."

"That's right," said Abby Cadabby. "My aunt says going to the dentist makes you feel better. And she's the tooth fairy, so she should know!"

"Wait! Elmo has an idea," said Elmo. "Abby can do magic! She could make a toothache go away with her training wand."

"I can't poof away a toothache, Elmo," said Abby. "I can only turn things into pumpkins. See?" And she waved her wand at a soccer ball: "Lumpkin, bumpkin, diddle-diddle dumpkin, zumpkin, frumpkin, PUMPKIN!!!"

Big Bad jumped nervously as the soccer ball turned into a pumpkin. "Elmo was right," said Big Bad. "I need a dentist—not magic."
"When Big Bad goes to the dentist, Elmo will go with him," Elmo said.

So, the next day, the Big Bad Wolf, Elmo, and Elmo's mommy all went to see Dr. Bradley. In the waiting room, Elmo saw lots of picture books and toys—even an aquarium!

"Ah-oowoooooo!" Big Bad yowled every now and then.

His toothache was only a teeny bit worse, but he was a wolf and couldn't help himself.

"The dentist will make your tooth better," Elmo's mommy said gently.

"Big Bad Wolf!" called the dental assistant, Miss Stella.
Big Bad whimpered, and Elmo felt worried about his friend.
"We'll take good care of him," Miss Stella told Elmo. "But why don't you come along and keep him company?"

"Good idea!" Elmo agreed. "Elmo can't wait to see how the dentist takes care of wolf teeth!"

Miss Stella smiled. "We take care of Big Bad Wolf teeth the same way we take care of little red monster teeth."

"Elmo, let's pretend you're having a check-up, so Big Bad can see what happens," said Miss Stella. "Climb up in the dentist's chair and I'll give you a ride."

"Woooo, Elmo is floating," said Elmo, as the chair s-l-o-w-l-y rose.

"Now it's your turn, Big Bad," said Miss Stella.

"Will Big Bad get a bib?" Elmo said, remembering his last visit.

"A bib? A baby bib?!" barked the wolf. "Whattaya mean? I'm too BIG! It says so right in my name."

Elmo giggled. "No, silly! It's to keep Big Bad from getting messy when Miss Stella cleans his teeth."

"And I wear a mask and gloves to protect little monsters—and big bad wolves—from germs," added Miss Stella.

Big Bad lay back in the chair, and Miss Stella pulled down a light. "It's pretty dark in there," Elmo said.

"Holy molars!" Miss Stella joked. "What big teeth you have!"

"Now," she added seriously, "we take X-rays—little pictures of your teeth. Then we brush your teeth to chase away any sugar bugs."

"Bugs?" Elmo exclaimed. "Like in Oscar's trash can?!? Ewwwww!"

"I mean things like sugar that might start a cavity—a little hole in your tooth. They're not really bugs," Miss Stella laughed.

"Ah ew at," mumbled Big Bad. (That's what "I knew that" sounds like with your mouth open wide.)

"Let's pick a yummy toothpaste," said Miss Stella. "What flavor do you like, Big Bad—cinnamon, peppermint, or bubblegum?"

"Ubbleum!" gurgled the wolf with his mouth still open.

"I'll put the toothpaste on this little brush and then we'll tickle your teeth," Miss Stella explained.

"A toothbrush that tickles your teeth. A toothbrush that tickles your teeth!" Elmo chanted. "Just saying that makes Elmo feel tickly all over!"

"Feel the brush on your paw—it's very soft," said Miss Stella. "We'll clean between the teeth with skinny string called floss. Then we'll rinse your mouth with a little squirty tool. And, before we're done, we'll look at your tongue and your gums."

"Wow," said Elmo. "That's a mouthful!"

Then Dr. Bradley, the dentist, came in. He gave Big Bad a pat on his shaggy head. "We'll get that tooth fixed right up," he said cheerfully. "Say, Elmo, tell me something: Does a train have teeth?"

"No." Elmo shook his head.

"Then how come it can CHOO?!?" Dr. Bradley hooted.

"Woof-woof-woof-woof!" chuckled Big Bad.

"I remember your first check-up, Elmo," said Dr. Bradley. "You were very little. You know, sometimes we even see tiny babies." Then he whispered: "But this is the first time we've ever had a wolf in the office."

"Ih mah fuh ahm, hoo," burbled Big Bad, meaning "It's my first time, too."

"My, what big ears you have," Dr. Bradley laughed.

Dr. Bradley asked Elmo to wait outside while he filled Big Bad's cavity. "Don't worry," he told Elmo. "I'll let your friend listen to some fun music while I fix his hurt tooth. How about Wailin' Jennings!"

When he was finished, Dr. Bradley called Elmo back in, and Big Bad proudly showed off his new filling.

"Now, Big Bad, I don't know what you've been eating," Dr. Bradley said kindly, "but it's given you a cavity."

Big Bad looked sheepish.

"So, from now on, be sure to eat lots of yummy, healthy foods, like cereal, vegetables, and fruit."

"Big Bad and Elmo like bananas!" said Elmo.

"Well, Big Bad, you're all done," said Dr. Bradley. "That filling will stop your toothache."

"Elmo wants to know what happens next, Dr. Bradley," said Elmo.

"Next, we find a time for Big Bad to come back for a check-up. That way, we can stop other cavities before they begin, and he can live happily ever after."

"Thank you, Dr. Bradley," said Elmo.
"Thank yooooooo!" loudly howled the wolf.
Elmo sighed. "Elmo wishes Big Bad wouldn't do that."

"Here are some new toothbrushes to take with you," said Miss Stella.
"And you get to pick something out of the treasure chest."
Elmo picked a wiggly, squiggly, play worm for his goldfish, Dorothy.
Big Bad Wolf took a toy tea set for Little Red Riding Hood.
"I'm not bad all the time," he told Elmo's mommy.

"Remember to brush for as long as it takes to sing your ABCs twice, in the morning and before you go to bed at night," Miss Stella said.
"Elmo and Big Bad promise," said Elmo. "Good-bye!"

The next day, Big Bad Wolf showed off his fangs to everyone.
"My, what big, healthy teeth you have," said Zoe.
"The better to EAT APPLES with!" Big Bad replied, as the
three little pigs scampered by.
"Look out!" they squealed gleefully. "He's after our apples!"
And away they raced—crying "wee, wee, wee," all the way home.

# WHERE IS ELMO'S FRIEND?

It's morning on Sesame Street! Everywhere you look, monsters are getting ready to start a bright new day.

Elmo wakes up ready for a happy morning. He looks around for his favorite doll, baby David . . . but baby David is missing!

Elmo feels worried and sad. He takes a deep breath and tries to remember where baby David was the last time he was lost.

Elmo remembers! Under the bed!

The only thing under Elmo's bed is his truck. But the truck gives Elmo a very good idea.

Yesterday, Elmo played with his truck AND baby David. If Elmo can remember all the things he did yesterday, he can find baby David!

Yesterday, Elmo wore his jacket and played outside in the sandbox.

Elmo checks the closet, but baby David isn't there. Elmo's jacket isn't either. Where should Elmo look next? Outside!

Uh-oh, baby David isn't in the sandbox. Where can he be? Elmo takes a breath to calm down. He remembers playing in the sandbox yesterday . . . and getting so sandy that Mommy had to wash his jacket.

Then Elmo sees his mom in the laundry room. Maybe . . .

. . . baby David is in the dryer!

Mommy helped Elmo take a bath last night. Now she's helping baby David clean up, too. Hooray! Elmo stayed calm and went back over his steps to find baby David—and he did!

"Thanks, Mommy!" says Elmo.
"Now baby David is all cuddly
and warm."
"So are you, sweetie,"
says Elmo's mom.
"Have a
wonderful day!"

# ELMO'S FIRST BABYSITTER

Elmo is so excited! Elmo is going to have a babysitter tonight! Her name is Emily. There's the doorbell! That must be Emily!

Um, wait a minute. Maybe Elmo doesn't really want a babysitter after all.

It *is* Emily. She looks nice, doesn't she? Elmo's mommy and daddy wrote down some helpful phone numbers. Now it is time to hug Mommy and Daddy good-bye.

Restaurant
555-9423

Neighbors
555-1616
555-8003

Did you see what we made? Kooky faces!
Elmo made this one all by himself!

Wow! Elmo likes this music!

Elmo's toe feels all better now. And look—Emily brought bubbles for Elmo to play with in the bathtub. When Mommy and Daddy give Elmo a bath, we don't ever get to blow bubbles.

Good morning, Mommy! Good morning, Daddy!
Elmo liked having a babysitter! It was fun!
When is Emily coming back?

It was getting dark, so the campers headed inside the tent to settle in for the night.

"Let's play another game," said Zoe. "I'm too excited to sleep!"

"I know," said Grover. "Let us make cute, furry animal shadows. Zoe, you hold this incredibly heavy flashlight while I, Grover, make shapes with my fingers. Just a smidge closer, okay? Okay."

"A ghost!" Grover exclaimed. "I do not like it when strange things fly through the air (unless, of course, it is a superhero). Ghosts are spooky. Oh, I am so scared!"

The friends huddled tightly together.

"WHOO-WHOO! WHOO-WHOO!"

Then, Zoe looked up and saw two bright eyes and big wings against the sky. "Whoa, wait a minute . . . that's not a ghost. Look, it's Hoots the Owl!"

Everyone breathed a big sigh of relief.

"Wow, we should find Grover and Zoe," said Big Bird.
"COME OUT, COME OUT, WHEREVER YOU ARE!"
    The two little monsters came running.
    "I knew you would not find us!" said Grover proudly. "We heard you
call and call, but then you gave up."
    "That wasn't me," replied Big Bird. "It was a ghost!"

"I know," Big Bird decided. "It must be Elmo trying to tell me where he's hiding."

So he followed the sound . . . and there was Elmo, peeking out from behind a tree.

"Elmo, were you making that strange sound?"

"No," said Elmo, in a small voice. "Maybe it's a ghost!"

Then Big Bird heard a strange sound: "Whoo-whoo!"

He stood still and listened very carefully. "Oh, that's just my echo," he said, and went back to looking for his friends.

"Whoo-whoo!" There it was again!

Big Bird's eyes opened wide. "Hey, that wasn't my echo. I didn't holler 'yoo-hoo' that time!"

The campers began playing hide-and-seek, and Big Bird was It. Grover, Zoe, and Elmo ran and hid.

"Eighteen, nineteen, twenty . . . ready or not, here I come! Yoo-hoo!" Big Bird called as he looked for his friends. Grover . . . Zoe . . . Elmo! Yoo-hoo!"

Everybody climbed inside to set up for the night. Soon all the sleeping bags were unrolled.

Big Bird tucked Radar into bed, and Elmo made sure his pet goldfish, Dorothy, was fed.

"It's too early to go to sleep," said Zoe, as she raced outside. "Let's play a game. It'll be neat!"

It was a great night for a sleep-out!

There was a full moon, and it wasn't cold at all.

"Elmo is so excited!" Elmo cried. "Sleep-outs are fun!"

"Come on in, everybody," said Zoe, who had been setting up her sleeping bag in the tent. "This is cool! We can look at the stars and tell stories!"

"This tent doesn't look very big," said Big Bird. "Do you think it will hold everyone?"

"Don't worry," said Zoe. "There's plenty of room!"

# ELMO'S SPOOKY SLEEP-OUT

"Now, what animal is this?" asked Grover. The shadow looked like a bear. And when Grover moved his fingers, the bear's mouth appeared to be moving.

Crunch-crunch-crunch-crunch.

"How does Grover make that crunching noise?" asked Elmo. "It sounds just like a bear eating."

"I do not know," said Grover slowly. "Th-that sound is not me!"

"Gee," said Big Bird, "it must be something with awfully big teeth."
"Maybe it's a huge hungry dragon!" said Zoe, creeping deeper into her sleeping bag.

"I have never seen a hungry dragon before, and I do not think I want to. But everything is fine," said brave little Grover in a shaky voice. "Do not worry."

CRUNCH-CRUNCH-CRUNCH-CRUNCH.

"The sound's getting closer," whispered Big Bird.

It was right outside! The tent flap began to rustle.

"Yikearoni! It's coming inside!" yelled Zoe.

A furry little face poked through the flap.

"BABY BEAR!" Big Bird shouted.

"Sorry I'm late," Baby Bear said brightly. "The fall leaves are just right for crunching while you walk. Hey, this tent is the perfect place to spend the night."

Baby Bear yawned, unrolled his sleeping bag, and dropped off to sleep.

Soon, everyone's eyes were drooping.

"I have never seen a hungry dragon before, and I do not think I want to. But everything is fine," said brave little Grover in a shaky voice. "Do not worry."

CRUNCH-CRUNCH-CRUNCH-CRUNCH.

"The sound's getting closer," whispered Big Bird.

It was right outside! The tent flap began to rustle.

"Yikearoni! It's coming inside!" yelled Zoe.

That's when Big Bird heard another peculiar sound:
Pant-pant-pant. Pant-pant-pant.

   "Those other noises were just Hoots the Owl and Baby Bear,"
he said to Radar—and himself. "This one won't be scary either."

   Pant-pant-pant. Pant-pant-pant. It was getting nearer!

   "Did you hear that?" Zoe whispered. Now everyone
was wide awake—except Baby Bear, who seemed to be hibernating.

Pant-pant-pant. Pant-pant-pant.
They heard it again.
"Maybe it's a witch who has just flown down on her broomstick!"
Elmo cried. "Please, please, please don't be a witch!"

"Oh, my goodness, I think you are right, Elmo," said Grover.
"It is a scary witch, with a green face and a tall pointy hat.
I wish my mommy would come!"
The tent flap was opening. The scary witch was almost inside!

Pant-pant-pant. PANT-PANT-PANT!

Suddenly, there in the opening was a pink tongue and a furry nose.

"Come on in, Barkley," giggled Zoe.

"Woof-woof!" Barkley answered, sniffing around happily and then curling up in the middle of the tent.

"There can't possibly be anything else out there," said Big Bird, and the friends nestled back into their sleeping bags.

A little while later, however, another sound woke everyone up:
Clang-clang-clang. Clang-clang-clang.

"Oh, no! There is something else out there!" Big Bird exclaimed.
"What clangs like that?"

"It can't be a ghost or a dragon or a witch," Elmo said.
"It must be a goblin!"

"EEK! A goblin!" everyone shrieked.

The clanging noise got louder.

Then Big Bird sniffed the air. "Hey, wait a minute. Do goblins smell like sardines?"

"This one sure does," replied Zoe.

CLANG-CLANG-CLANG!

The strange sound—and the smell—came closer.

"Hey, in there," said a gruff voice just outside the tent. "Knock off the noise. Can't a grouch get a little peace and quiet around here?"

"That's not a goblin," said Big Bird. "It's Oscar!"

Oscar the Grouch clanked inside.

"Grouches don't usually like sleep-outs," he scowled. "But this tent is disgustingly crowded, cramped, and noisy—so it's okay. I think I'll stay."

Suddenly, Zoe noticed a huge shadow on the side of the tent.
"L-l-look," she said, pointing nervously toward the opening.
Clomp-clomp-clomp came the sound of footsteps.
"It looks like a giant furry creature," said Big Bird.
Clomp-clomp-clomp!
The shadow grew bigger and bigger.

"It is the Abominable Bigfoot, and it is coming closer!" yelled Grover. "Oh, save us, Mommy! M-O-M-M-M-E-E!"

Slowly, the creature pulled back the tent flap, and . . .

. . . there was Grover's mommy!

"How about a midnight snack?" she asked, setting down a tray of milk and cookies.

"Oh, silly me," Grover said sheepishly. "There is really nothing scary out here in the backyard at all."

"That's right," Big Bird said with a yawn. "Can we finally go to sleep now?"

"Sleeping out really is fun," said Elmo, munching on a pumpkin spice cookie. "Even spooky sleep-outs!"

# ELMO AND THE BUTTERFLY ESCAPE

This is Elmo's school, one of Elmo's favorite places. Elmo loves reading . . . and counting . . . and when something silly happens.

Because something silly always happens when Elmo's at school. You'll see!

Oooh, look! Look outside the window! **One, two, three** butterflies flutter by.

One butterfly flutters **inside**! See, Elmo knew something silly would happen. Hi, butterfly!

Don't you think that flying looks like fun?
In school, Elmo learns to use his brain, so now
Elmo imagines what it would be like to fly.

Flutter-flutter.

Flutter-flutter.

Flutter-flutter.

Oops! While Elmo was flying in his imagination, he dropped his ball! It's bouncing awaaaay!

OOPS!

Elmo wonders . . . can you guess what silly thing might happen next?

Elmo's ball keeps bouncing and . . . uh-oh! Elmo's ball knocked down Zoe's blocks. Down they go!
Can you guess what silly thing might happen next?

Look! Elmo's toy dump truck rolls up and catches all the tumbling blocks!

A truck sure is a handy thing to have around. But Elmo's truck doesn't stick around. It rolls and rolls and rolls. Elmo's truck rolls too fast for Elmo to catch it.

Can you guess
what silly thing might
happen next?

Oh no! It's a good thing Fluffy's so fluffy.
The bump didn't hurt her one bit. But it did knock the cage door open.

Oh no!

At first, all Elmo sees is the butterfly,
fluttering by the bookshelf.
Do you see Fluffy anywhere?

Wow, look at Fluffy go! Elmo didn't know that little Fluffy's legs could move so fast.

Make way for **super-speeeeedy** Elmo!

Whoa! Elmo might have been going too fast! Elmo tripped on a cushion and is about to bump into the bookshelf.

Hmmm, the books on the shelf are leaning a little bit.
Whoa! There go all the books, right on top of the vase!

Can you guess what silly thing might happen next?

There goes the vase . . .
but Elmo catches it!

There go the flowers!
Good catch, Zoe!
Yay! Only a drop or two of
water got dripped.

Hey, do you hear that? No? Elmo can't hear anything either.
Because it's all quiet! Nothing is bouncing, tumbling, rolling,
running, slipping, tipping, or dripping.

Boy, all this quiet is making
Elmo a little bit sleepy.
It's a good thing it's rest
time now. Elmo will
rest on the rug, take
a quick nap, and
look for Fluffy
a little later.

Hmmm, the rug looks
lumpy and bumpy.

Can you guess what silly
thing might happen next?

Elmo doesn't believe this! It's Fluffy! She was snug as a bug under the rug . . . but now she's on the run again!

Here, Fluffy, Fluffy, Fluffy. Do you see her? Hey, what's that poking out of the playhouse?

It's Fluffy's little pink nose! A hamster's nose is pretty tickly.

Everyone is so happy that Elmo found Fluffy. Let's make some music to celebrate! Look, even the butterfly is dancing along!

See, something silly always happens when Elmo is at school. But did you guess how *many* silly things would happen today? And all because of one little butterfly.

Bye-bye, butterfly.
**Flutterby home!**

School's over, but can you think of something silly that might happen tomorrow?

# ELMO SAYS ACHOO!

Today Elmo's visiting his grandma and grandpa. Elmo's so happy that you're visiting, too.

Ding- dong!
Ding- dong!

Oooh—someone is ringing the doorbell! Elmo loves that sound. Ding-dong, ding-dong! But who could it be? Wow, it's the mailman with a package! Thank you, Mr. Mailman. Bye-bye. Have a nice day!

That's funny. Elmo's nose is starting to tickle. But there are no feathers or dandelions near Elmo's nose. Why is Elmo's nose so tickly?

Elmo wiggles and twitches and sniffles, but nothing will stop the tickle.

Uh-oh, now Elmo can't help himself. **Ah . . . . ah . . . .**

ACHOO!

Excuse Elmo, please.

Maybe something outside is making Elmo sneeze. Elmo will take a shortcut through the grocery store.

Hey, there's Elmo's friend, Bert. Hi, Bert!

Bert is stacking cans, neat and tall, one by one.

One can. **Ah...** Two cans. **Ah...ah...** Three cans.

**Ah...ah...ahhh...**

# ACHOO!

Whatever is making Elmo sneeze outside is making Elmo sneeze inside, too.

Boy, this sneezing is slowing Elmo down. Elmo better hurry past this busy barbershop. How much fun would Elmo have getting his hair cut?

Uh-oh. Elmo had better grab his hanky.

Ah... ah... ah...

Sesame Street is not far away now. Elmo can't wait to get to Oscar's can to see what's inside this package.

But first Elmo has to pass this long brick wall. It looks brand-new. The bricklayers ask Elmo to look at all the neat bricks. Elmo can see they are very proud of their work.

The wall is very nice and strong. But now Elmo feels another tickle.

Ah... ah...

# ACHOO!

Okay, that's it! Elmo really wants to know, what is *SO SNEEZY* around here?

Hey, what's that sound? Not ah-ah-achoos, but root-a-toot-toots. Look, look, look—here comes a parade!

Elmo wants to watch the elephants march and the super-tall monsters juggle and the colorful clowns make a pyramid.

Ah...

But Elmo can't forget that he has to deliver Oscar's package and—

Okay, this is TOO MUCH sneezing! It is time to deliver this package to Oscar the Grouch. Let's see if Oscar is home.

Knock-knock. Elmo likes that sound, too.

Knock-knock-knock, knock-knock, knock-knock, knock-knock!

Yoo-hoo, Oscar, Elmo knows you're in there. Elmo has a package for you. Don't you want to see what's inside, Oscar? Elmo does!

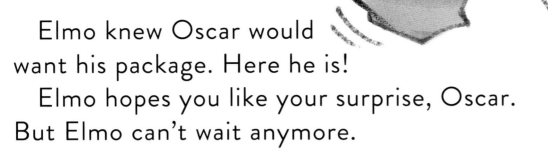

Elmo knew Oscar would
want his package. Here he is!
Elmo hopes you like your surprise, Oscar.
But Elmo can't wait anymore.

Elmo wants to know

# RIGHT THIS MINUTE what it is.

So does Bert. And the barber.
And the bricklayers. And the clowns.
So does Elmo's friend who's reading this book.

# Ewwwwwww!

A stinkweed plant!

Elmo can't believe his eyes.

Or Elmo's nose.

That stinkweed plant really stinks! Oscar says it's the best stinkweed plant he's ever sniffed.

Elmo is glad. Now Elmo's hanky can have a rest from all that sneezing. Oscar takes a big sniff. Elmo thinks it might be a good idea for Oscar to have a tissue, too. Here's one. Oscar will need it. Oscar sniffs one more big sniff. Then he itches. And he twitches. Uh-oh.

ACHO

Elmo thinks **YOU** can guess what happens next!

# MOMMY LOVES ELMO

Every night, Elmo snuggles into bed and waits for his favorite time of day. That's the time when his mommy sings him a lullaby.

Elmo loves his lullaby because it's all about how much his mommy loves him.

*Who loves Elmo? Who loves Elmo?*
*I love you. I love you.*
*Mommy's little monster,*
*sleepy little monster,*
*snuggle bug.*
*Hug, hug, hug.*

Even in the sunshine, Elmo remembers his mommy's lullaby. "Elmo loves you, Mommy," Elmo says.

"Elmo loves you because you sing Elmo bedtime songs and make Elmo yummy breakfasts. And Elmo loves you for all the other things that you do that Elmo is too hungry to remember right now!"

"Well, I love you too, Elmo," says Elmo's mommy.

"You do!" says Elmo. "But . . . how much do you love Elmo?"

"Would you love Elmo even if Elmo were a giant?" asks Elmo.
"I would love you even if you were a giant," says Elmo's mommy.
"I would love you no matter what!"

"Would you love Elmo even if Elmo were polka-dotty?" asks Elmo.
"Yes, I would love you even if you were polka-dotty," says Elmo's mommy.

"Would you love Elmo even if he had corners?" asks Elmo.

"I would love you even if you had corners," says Elmo's mommy. "I'd love my monster no matter what. I would even sing you a special song."

Who loves Elmo? Who loves Elmo?
I love you. I love you.
Mommy's little monster,
square-shaped little monster.
Huggable, lovable.

"You sing the best songs, Mommy," says Elmo. Then he stretches out his arms. "Elmo loves you thiiiiiiiiis much!"

"I know you do, Elmo," says Elmo's mommy. "But would you love me even if I sang just like the sound of a yucky old garbage truck?"

"Of course Elmo would!" says Elmo. "Elmo would love Mommy no matter what!"

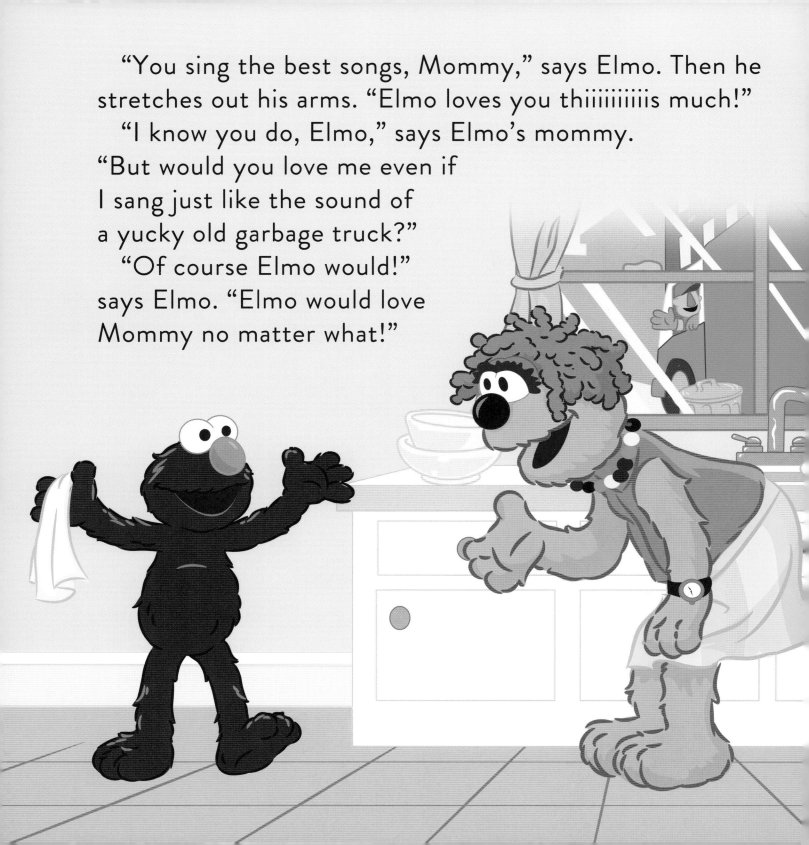

"Elmo, would you love me even if I were a cactus?" asks Elmo's mommy.

"Of course Elmo would love Prickly Mommy!" says Elmo. "Would Mommy love Elmo even if Elmo were a porcupine?"

"Of course I would love my porcupiney little monster," says Elmo's mommy.

"Hmm. Would you love me even if I were invisible?" asks Elmo's mommy.

"Of course Elmo would love Invisible Mommy," says Elmo. "But would Mommy love Elmo if Elmo were the size of a mouse?"

"Of course! I would love my little monster no matter what," says Elmo's mommy.

"Mommy . . . does Elmo have to wait till bedtime to hear Elmo's lullaby again? How about we sing a song right now? Together, Elmo and Mommy."

"Of course I would love to sing a song with my little monster," says Elmo's mommy.

Who loves Elmo?
Who loves Mommy?
Mommy does.
Elmo does.
He's her little monster.
She's his loving mommy.
Hug, hug, hug.
Hug, hug, hug.

# ELMO'S BAND

Elmo and Zoe are tidying up Sesame Street. This cleaning crew is being kind to their neighbors! And look what they find . . .

"Oooh, instruments!" Elmo says. "Let's make music."

"Yay! I love music," says Zoe, "because I love to dance!"

Elmo gets a **big** idea.

"Elmo wants to start a band. Does Zoe want to play?"
Elmo asks Zoe.

"Yes!" Zoe says. "Let's practice every day."

"Practice makes p-p-p-perfect,"
Elmo sings into his pretend microphone.

"Uh-oh," says Elmo. "This guitar has only five strings. It needs one more."

At the Fix-It Shop, Elmo counts: "One, two, three, four, five . . . **six**. Six strings all together!"

"It's a good thing you fixed your guitar," says Zoe.
"We have a concert tonight! Let's load up our big bus . . . "

"... and ride all the way to the show," Elmo adds. "Wheeeeee!"

Zoe imagines all the people taking pictures.
"Say cheese!" says Elmo.
"I'll **dance** up the red carpet," says Zoe.

"Elmo will **hop** up the red carpet," says Elmo.
"Elmo loves to hop-hop-hop!"

"The theater looks so **big** from here," says Zoe.
"And **empty**, too," says Elmo. "Where are all the people?"

"The theater looks so **big** from here," says Zoe.
"And **empty**, too," says Elmo. "Where are all the people?"

"Stuffed animals love music," says Zoe.

"Bravo, you found a really crummy audience," says Oscar.

"Now **scram**!"

Zoe laughs. Oscar is so silly!
"Now our band just needs a **name**," she says.
Elmo has an idea . . .

"Ladies and gentle-monsters," says Elmo, pretending to be an announcer. "Put your hands, paws, and claws together for **The Cleaning Crew**!"

# LOVE, ELMO

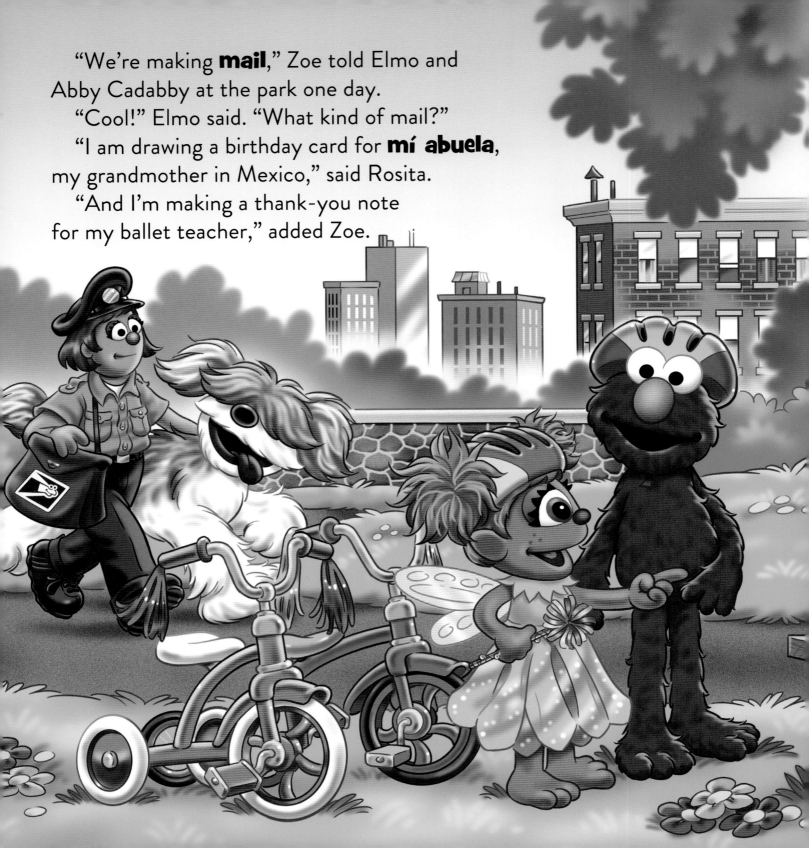

"We're making **mail**," Zoe told Elmo and
Abby Cadabby at the park one day.

"Cool!" Elmo said. "What kind of mail?"

"I am drawing a birthday card for **mí abuela**,
my grandmother in Mexico," said Rosita.

"And I'm making a thank-you note
for my ballet teacher," added Zoe.

"Ooh . . . those are so magical!" exclaimed Abby. "I've never had my very own letter before! Do fairies-in-training get mail?"

"I'm not sure," said Zoe. "But we have crayons and glittery stickers and markers. Want to make one?"

"Thanks, but I have to poof myself home now," said Abby. "My mommy says we're visiting Red Riding Hood's grandmother— or maybe it's the wolf. I can't remember."

"Abby has never ever gotten a letter before," Elmo told his goldfish, Dorothy, that night. "And Abby would like to have a letter of her very own. Wait a minute! Elmo can make a letter for Abby!"

So Elmo found some paper and crayons and asked his mommy for help. Mommy wrote two words at the top:

DEAR ABBY

"What comes next?" Elmo wondered.

"Something from your heart," said Mommy, giving him a hug.

"What do you think would make Abby happy?"

The next day after school, Elmo asked his friends for help.
"What was in Zoe's thank-you note?" Elmo asked Zoe.
"A picture of the Sugar Plum Fairy!" she answered.
"We're learning **The Nutcracker** ballet."

"Can Zoe draw the
Sugar Plum Fairy for Abby?"
   "Okay!" Zoe said, twirling on her toes.
"Abby will love the Sugar Plum Fairy.
   She wears a fluffy pink tutu and a sparkly tiara!"

"If it's fluffy and sparkly you want, how about a picture of Little Murray Sparkles?" suggested Telly.
"She's perfect for a fairy like Abby!"
"Thank you, Telly," said Elmo. "Would Baby Bear like to draw something on Abby's letter, too?"

Boing Boing

"Hmmm . . . I shall draw Cinderella's enchanted carriage,"
declared Baby Bear, "because Cinderella's fairy godmother created it
with a magic spell."

"Good idea!" said Telly. "And how about Cinderella on a pogo stick?"

"Pogo stick?!" asked Elmo.

"Sure," Telly said. "Who wants a carriage when you can **boing**
your way to the ball?"

Later that day, Elmo carried Abby's letter to Nani Bird's tree.
"Oh, hello, Elmo," said Big Bird. "We're practicing our hopping. Now remember, Birdketeers, if you want to get better at something, it's important to practice. Keep hopping! I'll just stand over here and be quiet. You won't hear a tweet out of me!"

"Elmo is making a letter for Abby," Elmo explained.
"Would Big Bird like to write something?"

"Sure, Elmo. Come on, everybody," Big Bird called.
"Let's help write a letter to Abby!"

The Birdketeers drew pictures of daisies, stars, and butterflies—
things a fairy might like. And Big Bird wrote a big A and C.

"A is for Abby and C is for Cadabby," he said proudly.

On his way to Bert and Ernie's, Elmo passed Oscar's trash can. "Can Oscar help make a letter for Abby?" Elmo asked.

"I can, but I won't!" Oscar scowled. "Wait a minute. Maybe if I do, little Miss Fairy Dust might wave that training wand of hers and fix my Sloppy Jalopy. Here, gimmee that paper, fur face. Let's see now, Abby likes pumpkins, right?"

"Ooh, Abby loves pumpkins!" Elmo said.

"Well, this one's nice and rotten," Oscar chuckled. "Now scram! I gotta give Slimey his mud bath. And, hey, don't tell anybody I drew that!"

"Okay, Oscar," giggled Elmo. "Have a rotten day!"

"Yeah, yeah," Oscar muttered. "Maybe it'll rain."

"Did I hear someone say **rain**?" asked Super Grover. "That is not good for swirly, adorable superhero capes!"

"Could Super Grover help make a letter for Abby?" Elmo asked.

"A letter? A **letter**? How about the letter **G**?" said Super Grover excitedly. "It has been very useful for this superhero."

And Super Grover scribbled a big, red letter **G**.

"Now if you will excuse me, I have super-hero deeds to perform and monsters to save," he proclaimed. "Clear the runway! Up, up, and away!"

"Thank you," yelled Elmo. "Super Grover was super helpful!"

At 123 Sesame Street, the Twiddlebugs were having a picnic in Bert and Ernie's windowbox.

"Elmo is making a letter for Abby," Elmo said. "Would Bert and Ernie like to add something?"

"Gee, that sounds like fun, doesn't it, Bert?" asked Ernie. "Let's see, I'll draw a picture of Rubber Duckie and me playing hide and squeak."

"And I'll write down my favorite bird joke," said Bert. "That'll make Abby laugh!"

What's a pigeon's favorite holiday?

Feathers' Day!

When Elmo got to Prairie Dawn's house,
everyone was practicing a play for
Try-A-New-Food Day.

"Take it from the top!" Prairie shouted.
"Oh, Elmo! We really need you to be a mango!"

"Elmo can be a mango tomorrow," Elmo said.
"But Elmo is making a letter for Abby today."

"Oh, wait, wait! Me know something to put in letter!"
Cookie Monster exclaimed. "It big and round and brown,
and it start with letter **C**!"

"Cookie Monster," Prairie sighed.
"Everybody **knows** it will be a picture of a cookie!"

"That what you think," said Cookie, drawing . . . a cantaloupe!

"It brown on outside and orange on inside," explained
Cookie Monster. "Tasty anytime treat!"

Elmo thought and thought as he walked home on Sesame Street. What could Elmo put in Abby's letter? Abby liked rhyming words— words that sounded the same, like **house** and **mouse** or **play** and **day**. She liked Mother Goose and the Storybook School. . . .

"Greetings!" said Count von Count, appearing suddenly.

"Mr. Count? Elmo has a question," Elmo said. "Elmo wants to put something in a letter to Abby, but how does Elmo pick just one thing?"

"Why would you want to pick just one thing?" asked the Count. "Choose two things, three things, ten things—twenty wonderful things! **Ah ah ah**! Just think of all the possibilities!"

That night, Elmo made up his mind. He drew a special picture on Abby's letter.

Then his daddy helped Elmo write a word at the bottom of the page.

Finally Elmo printed his name, nice and s-l-o-w.

And the next day, Abby got her very first letter. She was happy to see all the words and pictures from her friends on Sesame Street. And at the bottom of the page, she read . . .

DEAR ABBY,

A
C
G

What is a pigeon's favorite holiday? Feathers' Day